little bee books

An imprint of Bonnier Publishing USA
251 Park Avenue South, New York, NY 10010
Copyright © 2018 by Bonnier Publishing USA
All rights reserved, including the right of reproduction in whole or in part in any form.
Little Bee Books is a trademark of Bonnier Publishing USA, and associated colophon is a trademark of Bonnier Publishing USA.

Library of Congress Cataloging-in-Publication Data
Names: Newton, A. I., author. | Sarkar, Anjan, illustrator.
Title: Aliens for dinner?! / by A.I. Newton; illustrated by Anjan Sarkar.
Description: First edition. | New York, NY: Little Bee, [2018] | Series: The alien next door; #2 |
Summary: Harris and Roxy visit Zeke's house after school, then Harris's parents invite Zeke's family to dinner, but trying to convince anyone that they are aliens only gets Harris grounded.
Identifiers: LCCN 2017023253 Subjects: | CYAC: Extraterrestrial beings—Fiction. | Ability—Fiction. | Family life—Fiction. | Friendship—Fiction. | Science fiction. | BISAC: JUVENILE FICTION / Readers / Chapter Books. | JUVENILE FICTION / Science Fiction. | JUVENILE FICTION / Action & Adventure / General. Classification: LCC PZ7.1.N498 Ali 2018 | DDC [Fic]—dc23
LC record available at https://lccn.loc.gov/2017023253

Printed in the United States of America LAK 0218
ISBN 978-1-4998-0562-8 (hardcover)
First Edition 10 9 8 7 6 5 4 3 2 1
ISBN 978-1-4998-0561-1 (paperback)
First Edition 10 9 8 7 6 5 4 3 2 1
ISBN 978-1-4998-0563-5 (ebook)

littlebeebooks.com
bonnierpublishingusa.com

THE ALIEN NEXT DOOR

ALIENS FOR DINNER?!

by A. I. Newton
illustrated by Anjan Sarkar

little bee books

TABLE OF CONTENTS

1
THE INVITATION

HARRIS WALKER RAN OUT onto the Jefferson Elementary School soccer field. It was Friday afternoon, and practice was about to begin.

Harris's best friend, Roxy Martinez, trotted up next to him.

"It was fun having Zeke over last weekend, right? I hope you're done with that 'Zeke is an alien' nonsense," she said.

Zeke was Harris's new next-door neighbor. He had only been at their school for a couple of weeks.

But Harris believed that Zeke was an alien—a real-life alien who somehow came here from another planet. Harris saw Zeke do things that would be impossible for any human kid to do, like move things with his mind, make rainbows suddenly appear in the science lab, and even balance on his fingertips.

"I did have fun. Zeke's a nice kid," Harris replied.

But I still think he's an alien, Harris thought.

Coach Ruffins blew his whistle.

"Okay, everyone, let's get this practice going!" he shouted.

Harris, Roxy, and rest of the players spent the next hour working on passing, shooting, and defense.

When the practice was nearly over, Harris saw Zeke walking onto the field. A soccer ball flew right toward the front of Zeke's head.

"Look out!" Harris shouted.

He watched in amazement as the ball changed direction, all by itself. It swung around Zeke's head and continued into the goal.

Harris turned to Roxy.

"Did you see that?!" he asked her, sure that she must have seen Zeke control the ball with his mind.

"Yeah," said Roxy, "the ball came so close to hitting Zeke's head! I'm glad he didn't get hurt."

Drats! Harris thought. *From her angle, it must have looked normal.*

"What's up, Zeke?" Harris asked casually as the three friends walked back toward the school.

"I just wanted to thank you again for a great time hanging out at your house, Harris," said Zeke. "And also to invite the both of you to my house tomorrow. We could hang out and play. And my parents are anxious to meet you."

"Sounds great!" said Roxy. She looked at Harris, waiting for him to accept, too.

This is the perfect opportunity to research Zeke's alien family, Harris thought. *I can finally find out what's behind those dark curtains and prove once and for all that he's an alien!*

"I'd love to come over, Zeke," Harris said, giving Roxy a look that said: *See? I don't think he's an alien anymore.*

"Great!" said Zeke. "See you tomorrow!"

ZEKE BURST THROUGH the front door of his house. "Xad! Quar! I have something to tell you," he shouted.

9

"I'm up here, Zeke," said his father, Xad.

Zeke looked up and saw his dad floating near the ceiling. He sat in a cross-legged position. A metal helmet rested on his head.

Xad then drifted down, landing on the floor.

"I was just mind-transferring some of my latest research," Xad explained. "Did you know that humans wear different shoes in the rain and snow than they do on a sunny day?"

"I guess they don't have *adap-a-fiber* here," said Zeke.

"What is it, Zeke?" Quar, his mother, called out. She appeared in a shimmering haze to them, holo-projecting her image. "I'm out in the garden."

"Harris and Roxy have agreed to come here tomorrow," Zeke said.

"That's great, Zeke," said Quar. "We are so glad that you made two new friends so quickly."

"Yes, and it will also be the perfect chance to do some research on humans—up close!" said Xad.

"Don't forget you have to be as 'human' as possible, too," said Zeke, crossing his arms. "I don't want my friends to wonder what you're doing."

"Don't worry, Zeke," said Quar. "We will be careful and respectful."

Zeke nodded, then settled down to mind-project his homework.

At the same time, next door in Harris's house, Harris told his parents about Zeke's invitation.

"That's wonderful!" said Harris's mom.

"Well, I'm just glad you've given up on that crazy alien stuff," said his dad.

Harris nodded to reassure his parents, but thought: *Tomorrow, I'm finally going to prove that Zeke really is an alien!*

3 ZEKE'S HOUSE

THE NEXT DAY, HARRIS AND
Roxy arrived at Zeke's house.

"Can I take your coats?" Zeke asked
them.

Harris looked around the front

hallway. He was surprised at how normal everything looked, almost like his own house. But when he started to slip off his coat, he felt someone take it from him. Zeke and Roxy were standing right in front of him.

So who took my coat?

Turning around, Harris saw a pair of mechanical hands extending from the wall. They grabbed his coat, then Roxy's, and pulled them into an open panel in the wall.

"What was that?" Harris asked.

"Cool! So high-tech!" said Roxy.

Before Zeke could respond, Xad and Quar joined them.

"Roxy, Harris, I'd like you to meet my Quar and Xad," said Zeke. "I mean . . . my mom and dad."

"It's a pleasure," said Quar. "You both have been very kind to Zeke."

Zeke noticed that Xad was staring at Roxy's sneakers. They were bright blue with orange laces.

He leaned in and whispered. "Xad, try to not be so obvious about studying my friends' clothes!"

"Why don't we have some lunch?" suggested Quar.

Everyone gathered at the kitchen table. The table had no legs. It was just a clear disk hanging in midair.

How does that work? wondered Harris. *This must be alien technology, too! How is Roxy not bothered by this?*

"So, Harris, Roxy, what do you like to eat?" asked Xad.

"Burgers and hot dogs!" replied Harris.

"I like sandwiches and burritos," said Roxy.

Xad and Quar looked at each other, worried. They mind-projected their thoughts to each other so no one else could hear them.

Can our food replicator create these Earth dishes? Xad thought.

I don't know. It is only set to create Tragas food, Quar replied.

Zeke overheard this conversation in his mind. He jumped up from the table.

"I'll take care of lunch!" he said.

Zeke walked over to what looked like a huge floor-to-ceiling refrigerator. He pulled open the door. What only Zeke could see was that behind the door was actually a panel of switches, buttons, and blinking lights—the Tragas Food Replicator 3000.

The Tragas Food Replicator 3000 can create any food you ask it to . . . as long as it's served on Tragas! Zeke thought. *I hope it can make something close to these Earth foods!* He began pushing buttons and entering commands.

Harris leaned over to see what Zeke was doing, but Roxy poked him in the shoulder.

"Don't be rude!" she whispered. "What someone else keeps in their fridge is *their* business!"

A few minutes later, Zeke returned to the table with his arms full.

Harris stared at the steaming plates of food. *How did Zeke heat those up in the fridge?* he thought.

"Why does the burrito have purple polka dots?" he asked. "And how come the hot dog is a big circle?"

"These are the Tragas versions of those foods," Xad said quickly.

Harris bit into his hot dog and was surprised. It tasted sweet, like a candy bar.

Roxy tasted her burrito. She looked at Harris, and her face scrunched up. He could tell that her burrito must have tasted as weird as his hot dog.

Roxy smiled at Zeke. "Well, it sure is different. But good!" she said.

When everyone finished lunch, Zeke stood up.

"Why don't we go to my room and play some games?" he suggested.

The three friends headed to Zeke's room.

I can't wait to see what kind of alien stuff he has in there! thought Harris.

PLAYTIME!

THE THREE FRIENDS
stepped into Zeke's room. *Wow, it looks
similar to my room*, Harris thought.
They all sat down on a couch.

"Want to play a game?" Zeke asked.

He pressed a button under the couch, and a large screen blazed to life on the ceiling. The three of them looked up at the screen, and Harris's jaw dropped.

"I thought you didn't have video games in Tragas," said Harris.

"Well, not like the ones we played at your house," Zeke said.

"I've never seen a screen like that!" Roxy said.

That's because it's alien technology! Harris thought.

"We have a lot of high-tech stuff in Tragas. This game is called *Monster Mania*. You battle all kinds of monsters. But here's the coolest part."

Instead of giving Harris and Roxy hand-held controllers, Zeke placed a helmet onto each of their heads, and then placed one on himself.

"You create and control your avatar onscreen with your mind, not your fingers!" said Zeke. "And the monsters you battle also come from your own mind."

Zeke's avatar was a giant bird. When a fire-breathing, three-headed dragon appeared, Zeke controlled his bird with his mind and defeated the dragon.

Roxy's avatar was a warrior with a sword, shield, and armor. She battled a T. rex, but the dinosaur quickly clobbered her.

"This is hard!" she said.

"Keep playing. You'll get the hang of it," said Zeke.

Harris's avatar was a superhero with bulging muscles and a long cape. He fought a cyclops who swung a big wooden club. Despite his superpowers, Harris's avatar was overcome.

An army of trolls soon rushed at the three avatars.

"Work together!" said Zeke. "If we focus our thoughts on each others' avatars, we can defeat these trolls as a team!"

Harris concentrated really hard. After a few seconds, his avatar began fighting alongside the others, and they soon defeated the trolls.

"Cool game, Zeke!" Harris said. He was so caught up in the fun that he had stopped thinking that this game—like Zeke—might be from another planet.

"How about a movie?" asked Zeke.

"Sure," said Roxy, removing her game helmet.

Zeke pressed another button. The screen spun around and around. When it stopped spinning, a movie started.

"*Danger in the Deep*!" said Zeke. "It's one of my favorites. And it's a 4-D holo-projection! You feel like you're in the movie."

"Let me guess," Harris said. "High-tech stuff from Tragas?"

"Yup," said Zeke, smiling, and then they settled in for the movie.

Harris suddenly felt himself surrounded by yellow water. A giant sea creature with twelve tentacles swam past him.

"Wow!" he said. "I feel like I'm at the bottom of the ocean!"

"I hope that sea monster doesn't bite me!" Roxy said.

When the movie ended, the three friends headed downstairs. It was time to go home. Zeke's parents met them in the hallway.

"Thanks for having us over," said Roxy.

But Xad didn't seem to hear her and instead pointed at the label on Harris's T-shirt.

"What is the purpose of this?" Xad asked.

That's really strange, Harris thought. *Who doesn't know what a shirt label is?*

"Um, it tells you the size and fabric, and how to clean it," Harris explained.

"Fascinating," said Xad, making notes on a tablet.

A panel in the hallway wall slid open. Out popped Harris's and Roxy's jackets.

"Thanks again!" said Roxy.

"Bye, Zeke!" said Harris as they headed out the door and walked back to Harris's house.

"What a cool house and family! He's a really nice kid, isn't he?" said Roxy. She got on her bike and rode away.

Harris couldn't believe she didn't comment on everything weird that happened there. *Yeah, it was fun, but based on the way-too-advanced tech, the crazy food, and Zeke's strange parents, he's definitely a nice* **alien** *kid!*

ZEKE JOINED HIS PARENTS in the living room. All three floated upside down in the air, up near the ceiling.

"I'm not certain it was wise to show your friends all that Tragas technology," said Xad.

"*You're* the one who was so obvious when you inspected their clothes!" Quar said.

"I think it's all okay," said Zeke. "Harris may still be a little suspicious, but he's the only one."

"Well, just be careful, Zeke," said Xad.

Zeke rolled his eyes. "It's fine, Xad."

Meanwhile at Harris's house, his parents wanted to hear all about his visit to Zeke's.

"I hope you were nice to Zeke," said his mom.

"Yeah, no more alien talk," added his dad.

"No, no, we just played some games, that's all," said Harris. *Games from another planet!* he thought. *Even if they were kind of fun . . .*

"Did Zeke's parents tell you anything about Tragas?" asked his dad. "I'm still surprised no one has ever heard of it."

"It's true. They're our new next-door neighbors, but we know so little about them," said his mom.

Harris saw a familiar expression coming across his mom's face. *Uh-oh,* he thought.

"Why don't we invite Zeke and his parents here for dinner?" asked his mom.

"What a great idea!" said his dad.

Harris was shocked. *The aliens . . . here?! Zeke is one thing, but the parents with their odd food and their strange questions? I can't believe Mom is serious!*

"Roxy can come, too," his mom added.

Hmm, Harris thought. *Maybe this isn't a bad thing after all. Maybe seeing Zeke and his parents doing weird stuff at my house, in front of my parents, will be the proof I need to get everyone to realize that Zeke really is an alien.*

"Sounds good, Mom," said Harris.

6 SHOWING OFF

HARRIS WAS LOOKING forward to having Zeke's family over for dinner. This would be his big chance to prove to his parents and Roxy that Zeke was an alien. The dinner was set for the following Saturday.

At school that week, Zeke almost seemed to be showing off.

In gym class, everyone had to climb
up a rope. Harris struggled to pull
himself even halfway up.

He glanced to his left and saw Zeke
scurrying up his rope—with his hands
behind his back!

"Wow! That kid sure has strong legs!" said the boy who was climbing the rope to Harris's right. Zeke smiled at Harris on his way down the rope after touching the ceiling.

Is he showing off? Harris wondered. *Could he be getting too confident now that I've been in his house, met his parents, and seen his Tragas technology?*

Later, during arts and crafts, Harris worked on building a birdhouse. He started gluing Popsicle sticks together. As he waited for some of them to dry, he looked over at Zeke and saw that he had already completed a big birdhouse. It had a hole cut in the front, a perch, and a completed roof. Harris had barely begun, and Zeke was already finished.

How did he do that so quickly? Harris wondered.

The next day, Harris was sitting in math class.

"Okay, class, here's your brain-buster problem for the day," said Ms. Milton, their teacher.

She proceeded to write a long list of four-digit numbers on the board. Then she wrote a five-digit number right below it.

"I'd like you to add this list of numbers together, then divide the result by the number on the bottom," said Ms. Milton.

Zeke's hand shot into the air.

"Yes, Zeke. Do you have a question?" asked Ms. Milton.

"No, Ms. Milton. I have the answer," Zeke said.

His fellow students giggled. Zeke looked around, puzzled. Then he told Ms. Milton the answer.

"Why . . . that's correct, Zeke," she said. "Very good! You certainly have a flair for math."

Should I be surprised that an alien's brain works faster than a human's? Harris thought. *I can't wait for Saturday night. Then everyone will finally know.*

7 THE VERY SPECIAL VISITORS

SATURDAY FINALLY CAME.
Harris was excited, but nervous. His parents would finally see for themselves how strange Zeke's family was.

He spent most of the day helping his parents clean the house and set up for dinner.

Roxy came over early to help.

"Now remember, Harris, you need to be on your best behavior," said his mom. "We want Zeke's family to feel welcome in the neighborhood."

"Nothing to worry about, Mom," said Harris, smiling.

Just then, a whistling sound came from outside their front door.

"What in the world is that?" asked Mr. Walker.

Harris remembered Zeke's first day at school. Zeke had whistled outside the classroom door instead of knocking.

"That's Zeke and his parents,"
Harris explained. "That's how people
knock in Tragas!"

Harris opened the door.

"Come in," he said to the three of
them as he suspiciously eyed the food
they were carrying.

Harris introduced everyone.

"Zeke, these are my parents," Harris said.

"Welcome," said Harris's mom, extending her hand. "Rita and Felix Walker. Nice to meet you."

Zeke's father stared at Mrs. Walker's outstretched hand. "I am Xad, and this is my wife, Quar," he said.

Xad extended his elbow toward Mrs. Walker.

"Um, Dad? People here don't touch elbows as a greeting," Zeke explained. "They shake hands."

"Oh, I'm sorry," said Xad, reaching out and grasping Mrs. Walker's hand firmly before shaking it.

"I kind of like the elbow thing," said Mr. Walker. He extended his elbow and touched Quar's elbow. They both smiled.

"Why don't we have some appetizers in the living room?" said Mr. Walker.

The whole group settled into the living room.

Harris's dad picked up a cracker and placed a slice of cheese on it.

"Cheese and cracker?" he offered Quar.

She took the appetizer and stared at it. When she saw Mr. Walker take a bite, she did the same.

"It tastes kind of sweet and crunchy," said Quar. "I like it. Oh, we brought a delicacy from Tragas to share with you. These are called kreslars."

Xad took the lid off of a platter, revealing what looked like glowing purple slugs.

"Are they raw?" Harris asked, a little grossed out by the slugs' slimy appearance.

"They are, but they don't have to be," replied Xad. "Try one, Harris."

Harris picked up a slug and noticed that steam was now coming off of it. It was warm to the touch.

How did they do that? he wondered. *How did they make it hot?*

"Interesting; they taste kind of like warm fruit," said Mr. Walker.

After trying one, Roxy smiled and looked at Harris. "Not bad, right?"

A buzzer rang in the kitchen, and Harris quickly put his slug back.

"Okay, everybody," Mrs. Walker announced. "Dinner is ready!"

8
DINNER WITH ALIENS!

THE DINNER GUESTS SAT down around the dining room table. Roxy and Harris carried steaming platters of food from the kitchen.

Zeke got up to help.

As Harris put down a platter of fish, he saw Zeke returning from the kitchen. Zeke balanced two bowls, three plates, and a pitcher of water on his arms, shoulders, and head—all quite easily. Harris's parents clapped.

"That's pretty impressive!" said Mr. Walker. Harris put his face in his hands.

"Zeke told us you move around a lot. You must have lived in some interesting places for your work," said Mrs. Walker.

"Oh, yes," said Quar. "In Plaxima, the weather was so severe that we had to walk backward so the wind didn't blow us over. In Jerstik, people could eat their clothing."

"And in Nanstu, the language was so complicated, just saying hello took five minutes," added Xad.

"I've never heard of any of these places," said Mrs. Walker.

"They are pretty far away, and very small," Zeke said quickly, shooting his parents an annoyed look. After all the warnings they gave him about keeping the truth hidden, here *they* were telling strange stories.

As he listened, Harris grew more convinced than ever that Zeke and his parents were aliens. He also noticed that platter after platter of food somehow appeared in front of Zeke and his parents. But he never saw anyone touch or pass anything to anyone else.

I could have sworn those potatoes were in front of Roxy a second ago, and now they're in front of Zeke!

Harris also saw that neither Zeke nor his parents used their utensils. He watched as the food subtly floated up from their plates to their mouths when no one else was looking.

Why doesn't anyone else see this? Harris wondered in frustration.

"What's that?" Roxy asked, pointing to a bottle of orange-and-green liquid that Zeke's parents brought.

"It is Saurlic, a popular beverage in Tragas," explained Xad. "Try some."

Roxy poured herself a glass and took a sip.

"Mmm . . . takes like a cross between lemonade and orange juice," she said. "I like it." Roxy quickly drank down the whole glass.

Harris looked away for a second to see what Zeke was up to. Zeke was only looking back at him, smiling. When he turned back to Roxy, her empty glass was full again!

How did that happen? he thought. *The bottle is all the way across the room. There is no way anyone could have brought it over, refilled Roxy's glass, then put it back in just a few seconds!*

When dinner ended, Mrs. Walker stood up.

"Let's move to the den for dessert and coffee," she suggested.

9

GROUNDED!

AS HIS PARENTS PREPARED dessert and Harris was walking toward the den, he spotted Zeke's parents in the front hallway. They were both leaning into the coat closet.

"Are you looking for something?" Harris asked.

Quar and Xad turned around quickly. The both looked embarrassed. In reality, they were researching the clothes in the closet. But they couldn't say that to Harris.

Zeke walked in and spoke up. "My parents left the dessert they brought in the closet," he said.

"That's right," said Quar. She reached back into the closet and pulled out a white cake with colorful frosting in a pattern of square shapes.

"Uh, great," said Harris. "You can just bring that into the den."

But Harris was suspicious. *This sounds fishy to me,* he thought. *They never even wore coats and had no reason to go into that closet! Why would they have put a cake in there?*

Harris joined the others in the den. He picked up a knife to cut a piece of the cake and noticed that the squares in the frosting had changed into a series of wavy lines.

Harris looked around. Everyone was chatting, sipping coffee, and happily eating dessert. Zeke and his parents were even using utensils now. It would have seemed perfectly normal if not for everything else Harris had already seen.

Why does no one but me ever seem to notice all the strange stuff that happens around Zeke and his family? he wondered. *The appetizer that suddenly cooked itself, the refilling glass, the food appearing magically in front of Zeke, Quar, and Xad, the changing cake frosting, not to mention everything that happened at Zeke's house and also at school. It's all too much. And yet nobody sees it but me!*

"Well, we would like to thank you for a lovely evening," Quar said when everyone had finished dessert. "But we should be getting home."

Quar, Xad, and Zeke all stood up.

This is it! Harris thought. *My best chance to prove that Zeke's an alien is about to end. I can't take it anymore. I have to convince them. They have to have noticed something. It's now or never!*

Harris stood up.

"That's it! The game is over, Zeke," he announced. "I know that you and your parents are aliens!"

Everyone looked horrified. Roxy looked at Harris and shook her head. Harris's parents jumped up from their seats. "Harris!!!" his mom said.

But Harris continued.

"With all the strange stuff that happened tonight—the floating trays of food, the refilling glass, the steaming appetizer, the—"

Harris's mother cut him off.

"THAT'S ENOUGH!" she shouted.

"Harris. You are grounded. Go to your room right now!"

"But—"

"Now!" his dad said. Defeated, Harris skulked upstairs.

He had his one shot and he blew it. He lingered at the top of the stairs and overhead the rest of the conversation.

"I don't know how to apologize for my son's behavior," said Mr. Walker.

"Don't worry," said Quar. "Our customs in Tragas are very different from yours. Misunderstandings like this happen all the time."

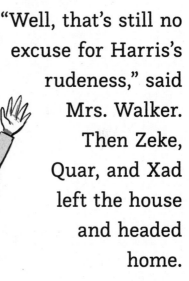

"Well, that's still no excuse for Harris's rudeness," said Mrs. Walker. Then Zeke, Quar, and Xad left the house and headed home.

"Harris just hasn't been his old self since Zeke showed up at school," Roxy said. "I'm worried about him."

"Well, he's lucky to have a friend like you," said Mrs. Walker.

When the cleanup was finished, Roxy went home. This disastrous dinner finally came to an end for all of them.

10 THE TRUTH AT LAST!

ZEKE WAS VERY UPSET.

"I can't believe Harris did that!" he said when he and his parents got home. "I knew he had his suspicions, but I never thought he would just blurt it out like that! I shouldn't have pushed him. . . ."

"Don't worry, Zeke," said Quar. "Most humans only believe these things up to a point."

"And even those closest to Harris think he's wrong," added Xad. "Forget about it. It'll go away. Anyway, this was very productive. I think our next research topic might be on strange human foods!"

But Zeke couldn't just let it go.

Harris is my friend, he thought. *And now he's in trouble, just because he was able to figure out the truth. I really like Harris. He and Roxy were the first kids to be really nice to me at school. Even if he was only nice to me to prove that I'm an alien, we have fun together, right? I feel terrible about this. And now Harris is grounded for who knows how long? But he wasn't wrong! He doesn't deserve to be in trouble.*

And I'm going to do something about it!

Harris remained grounded for the time being. He went to school each day, but then he had to come right home. He couldn't see his friends. He wasn't even allowed to talk to Roxy on the phone. And he was worried about what she must have thought of him after what happened.

A few days later at the dinner table, Harris said to his parents, "I apologize for being rude to our guests on Saturday."

"And are you ready to admit that what you said is nonsense?" asked his mother.

Harris stayed silent.

"Well then, it's back to your room as soon as you're finished with dinner," said his father.

The next day after school, Harris was stuck in his room as usual. He was bored. He had nothing to do except think about Zeke. Even his favorite comic books were taken away by his parents.

He rolled over on his bed and glanced out the window. There was Zeke floating in midair, two stories up!

Harris leapt from his bed and rubbed his eyes. When he opened them, Zeke was gone. He rushed to his window and looked outside, but there was nothing there.

"What the . . . ?"

Harris turned around and jumped up in surprise. Zeke was standing behind him, right there in Harris's room.

"How did you get in here?" Harris asked. "Is this even real? Am I dreaming? Have I lost my mind?"

"No, Harris," said Zeke. "You are awake . . . and sane. Well, as far as I know," Zeke said with a smile. "And you're correct."

"Correct?" asked Harris.

"My family and I really are aliens from the *planet* Tragas," Zeke admitted. "You are my friend, and I couldn't let you be grounded anymore for figuring out the truth."

Harris gasped and said, "I *knew* it!"

"My parents and I do move from place to place," Zeke explained. "But it is from planet to planet. I'm always the new kid. And I'm always 'different.' But you wanted to be my friend anyway."

"I don't know what to say," said Harris. "I'm glad you trust me. And am also glad I'm not crazy!"

"And now I must ask you to help me keep my secret," said Zeke. "Most people on Earth wouldn't be as welcoming as you."

"I will," Harris promised. "As long as you promise you're not one of those evil aliens I always see in the movies."

Zeke laughed and said, "Most of the time. I promise."

Zeke levitated into the air and floated out the window.

Harris raced downstairs.

"Mom! Dad!" he called out. "I have something to tell you."

His parents met him at the bottom of the stairs.

"I want to apologize," he said.

"I admit that I have an overactive imagination. I let it get the better of me. Of course Zeke and his parents aren't aliens. That was dumb. You'll never hear me mention it again."

"Well, I'm very glad to hear you say that, Harris," said his dad. "I think you can officially consider yourself un-grounded now."

His mom nodded in agreement. "As long as you go upstairs and call Zeke and his parents to apologize to them. And after that, call Roxy. You owe her an apology, too."

"I'll do it right now," said Harris.

He bounded up the stairs, excited by this new chance to help his new friend Zeke *keep* his secret rather than trying to expose it.

I was right! My next-door neighbor is actually an alien! He looked out his window where Zeke had been floating just a few minutes before and thought, *How cool is that?!*

Read on for a sneak peek at the third book in the Alien Next Door series!

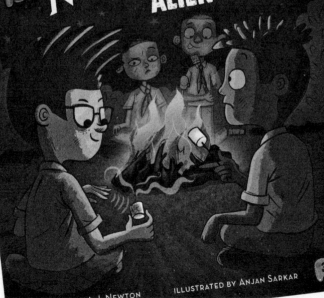

THE ALIEN NEXT DOOR

ALIEN SCOUT

3

BY A. I. NEWTON   ILLUSTRATED BY ANJAN SARKAR

1 A FRIEND'S SECRET

HARRIS WALKER AND HIS FRIEND ZEKE were sprawled out on the floor of Harris's bedroom, reading comic books. Harris loved showing off his collection.

"Now this one is called *Invaders From Beyond*," Harris said. "It's about these aliens from another dimension who can travel through time and shoot power beams from their eyes that can blow up entire mountains."

Zeke looked at his friend and laughed.

"You don't really believe all this stuff is true, do you?" he asked.

Harris laughed, too.

"Well, *you* can do some pretty amazing things, can't you?" he asked.

A lot had changed in the friendship between the two next-door neighbors since Zeke finally admitted the truth to Harris—Zeke was an alien from the planet Tragas!

"Yeah, but not *that* amazing," said Zeke. "Traveling through time and blowing up mountains is a bit beyond my skills."

"Okay, so what *can* you actually do?" Harris asked. "I mean, I know you can float, you can project what you see in your head onto screens, and you can heat stuff up with your hands."

"Let's see," Zeke said. "I can also move objects with my mind."

The next page in the comic book page turned over all by itself, revealing a picture of an alien lifting an entire building with one hand.

"Well, I definitely can't do *that*!" Zeke said.

Both boys laughed.

The next morning, Harris sat on the school bus next to Zeke.

"I just found out that I'm going on a camping weekend with the Beaver Scouts," Harris said excitedly.

"Beaver Scouts?" Zeke asked.

"They run this camp, and every October, boys can go there for a long weekend," Harris explained.

"I've heard people talk about it for years. In fact, my dad went when he was a kid. And this year, *I* finally get to go! We'll get to do all kinds of cool stuff—go canoeing, pitch a tent, and even tell scary stories at night!"

"And these things are fun?" Zeke asked.

Before Harris could answer, his best friend Roxy joined them on the bus.

"Well, you look pretty happy," she said to Harris.

"He is going to something called . . . Beaver Scout Camp," Zeke explained, still not quite sure what it was all about.

"So your parents finally think you're old enough to go? " asked Roxy. "Congratulations! I know how much you've looked forward to this. Is Zeke going, too?"

"No," replied Harris. *Actually, I don't think I know anyone who's going*, he thought to himself.

When the bus arrived at school, Harris pulled Zeke aside after they got off.

"Why don't you see if you can come with me to the camp?" he blurted out.

Even though he was excited, Harris was a little nervous about going off to camp and not knowing anyone else who'd be there.

"It'll be really fun, I promise, and a great way to learn about Earth kids!" said Harris.

"I guess it might be. . . ." said Zeke. "I'll talk it over with my parents."